Firefighters

A Level One Reader

By Cynthia Klingel and Robert B. Noyed

The Child's World®

When I grow up, I want to be a firefighter.

A firefighter must learn many things.

5

A firefighter must practice even when there is no fire.

A firefighter wears special clothes.

The clothes protect the firefighter from the fire.

At a fire, each firefighter has a special job.

Some firefighters rescue
people in the fire.

Other firefighters put out the fire.

17

Being a firefighter can be risky.

Firefighters help many people. I want to be a firefighter!

Word List

clothes

rescue

risky

special

Note to Parents and Educators

Welcome to The Wonders of Reading™! These books provide text at three different levels for beginning readers to practice and strengthen their reading skills. In addition, the use of nonfiction text gives readers the valuable opportunity to *read to learn*, not just to learn to read.

These leveled readers allow children to choose books at their level of reading confidence and performance. Level One books offer beginning readers simple language, word choice, and sentence structure as well as a word list. Level Two books feature slightly more difficult vocabulary, longer sentences, and longer total text. In the back of each Level Two book are an index and a list of books and Web sites for finding out more information. Level Three books continue to extend word choice and length of text. In the back of each Level Three book are a glossary, an index, and a list of books and Web sites for further research.

State and national standards in reading and language arts emphasize using nonfiction at all levels of reading development. The Wonders of Reading™ books fill the historical void in nonfiction for primary grade readers with the additional benefit of a leveled text.

About the Authors

Cynthia Klingel has worked as a high school English teacher and an elementary teacher. She is currently the curriculum director for a Minnesota school district. Writing children's books is another way for her to continue her passion for sharing the written word with children. Cynthia is a frequent visitor to the children's section of bookstores and enjoys spending time with her many friends, family, and two daughters.

Robert Noyed started his career as a newspaper reporter. Since then, he has worked in communications and public relations for more than fourteen years for a Minnesota school district. He enjoys writing books for children and finds that it brings a different feeling of challenge and accomplishment from other writing projects. He is an avid reader who also enjoys music, theater, traveling, and spending time with his wife, son, and daughter.

Published by The Child's World®, Inc.

PO Box 326
Chanhassen, MN 55317-0326
800-599-READ
www.childsworld.com

Photo Credits
© 1993 Aneal Vohra/Unicorn Stock Photos: 2
© 2000 DPA/Dembinsky Photo Assoc. Inc.: 21
© 2002 Frank Siteman/Stone: 14
© 2002 Gary Irving/Stone: 17
© G. I. Rothstein/Photri, Inc.: 10
© 2000 G. Van Frankenhuyzen/Dembinsky Photo Assoc. Inc.: cover
© 1996 John Mielcarek/Dembinsky Photo Assoc. Inc.: 13
© 2000 John Mielcarek/Dembinsky Photo Assoc. Inc.: 5, 9
© 1998 Mark E. Gibson/Dembinsky Photo Assoc. Inc.: 6
© 2002 Vince Streano/Stone: 18

Project Coordination: Editorial Directions, Inc.
Photo Research: Alice K. Flanagan

Library of Congress Cataloging-in-Publication Data
Klingel, Cynthia Fitterer.
Firefighters / by Cynthia Klingel and Robert B. Noyed.
    p. cm.
ISBN 1-56766-938-7 (library bound : alk. paper)
1. Fire extinction—Juvenile literature. 2. Fire fighters—Juvenile literature.
[1. Fire fighters. 2. Occupations.]   I. Noyed, Robert B. II. Title.
TH9148 .K55 2001
628.9'25'023—dc21
                          00-013172